New School, New Me!

J.M. Klein

An imprint of Enslow Publishing

WEST **44** BOOKS™

The **TOTALLY** SECRET DIARY of DANI D.

New School, New Me!
My Home Is a Battlefield
Star of the Show
Best Friends For-Never

Please visit our website, www.west44books.com.
For a free color catalog of all our high-quality books,
call toll free 1-800-542-2595 or fax 1-877-542-2596.

Cataloging-in-Publication Data

Names: Klein, J.M.
Title: New school, new me! / J.M. Klein.
Description: New York : West 44, 2019. |
Series: The totally secret diary of Dani D.
Identifiers: ISBN 9781538381953 (pbk.) | ISBN 9781538381960 (library
  bound) | ISBN 9781538382981 (ebook) Subjects: LCSH: Schools--
  Juvenile fiction. | Self-confidence in children-- Juvenile fiction. | Diaries--
  Juvenile fiction. | Friendship--Juvenile fiction.
Classification: LCC PZ7.K545 Ne 2019 | DDC [E]--dc23

First Edition

Published in 2019 by
Enslow Publishing LLC
101 West 23rd Street, Suite #240
New York, NY 10011

Editor: Theresa Emminizer
Designer: Seth Hughes

Printed in the United States of America

CPSIA compliance information: Batch #CS18W44: For further information contact
Enslow Publishing LLC, New York, New York at 1-800-542-2595.

The **TOTALLY** SECRET DIARY of

DANI D.

Sunday night, November 4

My dad says I am the bravest girl he knows.

That used to be true.

Last summer, I went down the tallest waterpark slide. *Three times.* Emily Grace would only go down the smallest. Also, I tried mint ice cream. Emily Grace said it looked like green goo. *And* I passed Ben Jenkins a note during science. Emily Grace wouldn't even talk to him.

But now I know I'm *not* the bravest girl. I think maybe I was only ever braver than Emily Grace.

Mom says secrets have a way of getting out—especially when you try to keep them to yourself. That's why I'm writing my secret down here. So it *can't* get out. No one can know.

Here is my secret. I am not brave. I'm starting a new school tomorrow, and I am scared. I can't even be braver than Emily Grace. My best friend is now five whole hours away.

This is a BIG problem. Dad can't find out about this. I *know* he would be disappointed in me. My dad is a police officer. He deals with bad guys and car accidents and everything. He's nothing *but* brave.

I wish Dad could hug me. I wish he could tell me everything will be all right. I wish he could make extra chocolaty brownies with me. But he can't even do that.

My dad is also five hours away.

"This is going to be a good thing," Mom said after dinner tonight. We were sitting in my grandparents' living room. "Really, Dani. Oak Grove Middle School is a better school than your old school. You could join so many different clubs. And it's twice as big as your old school. You'll have no problem making new friends."

Mom didn't get it. Twice as many students? That's THE ENTIRE PROBLEM. How am I supposed to make friends? School started two months ago. Everyone has already picked their friends. They already know where to sit at lunch.

I will be the only new girl.

I knew *everyone* at my old school. Emily Grace and I have been best friends *forever*. I met her in second grade! And no one cared if I got sad about my parents. Or if I did something silly or dumb. Jasmine and Kayla even thought I was funny.

My friends back home liked me.

Mom drove me by the new school yesterday. All the kids there seemed so much cooler than me. It was the way they were dressed. It was the way they stood. It was the way they all hung out in groups.

I am not cool. And I know it.

Later, I asked Mom, "Can't we just go back home? Please?"

Mom sighed and said, "Dani, we've talked about this."

I got up and went to the kitchen. I asked Grandma if I could make extra chocolaty brownies while video chatting with Dad. But Grandma said no. She had just cleaned the kitchen. (Grandma has always just cleaned the kitchen. Her kitchen is the cleanest kitchen I have ever seen.) And she told me I should only video chat my dad from my bedroom.

"Your mom needs space right now, Dani," she said.

And then she frowned.

Grandma frowns a lot now that Mom and I live here.

Grandpa does, too.

I went back to my new bedroom. But I didn't call Dad. I started writing in this diary. Dad gave it to me when Mom and I moved. I'm going to write down everything that I can't tell anyone. Everything in this diary is a *total secret*.

My parents are "taking a break." They might even ~~get a divorce~~ split up. I'm not supposed to visit my dad until next summer. I won't see Emily Grace for seven months.

I am on my own.

split

I *have* to make friends right away.

I have to pretend to be cool at my new school tomorrow. I have to pretend that I'm happy. That I have no worries. I was kind of dorky at my old school. NO ONE CAN KNOW THAT.

It's a new school. So I will have to be a new me.

I told a big lie today.

I didn't mean to. I know lying is bad. It just sort of...happened.

My first day at school started REALLY bad.

First, I wore the wrong clothes.

My clothes fit in at my old school. My bright green skirt is just like Emily Grace's yellow one. And the purple polka dots on my shirt match my friend Kayla's backpack.

All the kids at Oak Grove Middle School wear dark colors. Navy. Black. And lots and lots of gray. Everyone wears jeans. Not one person was in a skirt like me.

GRAY

Then the school counselor took a really long time giving me a tour. I was late to first period. All the kids looked up when I walked in.

"This is Dani," the counselor said. "Dani, this is Mrs. West."

Mrs. West is my new math teacher. But she didn't say anything about math. She frowned. "We already have a Danny in the class."

And then a boy in the back of the room said in a loud voice, "I'm not sharing a name WITH A GIRL."

And the entire class laughed!

Mrs. West hushed everyone. "Don't be silly. You can both keep your name."

She turned to me. "Dani, what's your last name?"

My last name is Donaldson. I told her that.

"Perfect!" Mrs. West said. "We will call you

Dani D. And Danny Morris, you can be Danny M."

It was NOT perfect. At least she didn't make me go by Danielle. Mom only uses my full name when I'm in trouble. But it's not fair that I have to share my name with Danny M. He is so ANNOYING. He spent the rest of the class getting other kids to laugh at me.

"What does the D stand for, Dani D.?" he said. "Dani Dork?" And then he laughed.

That was not going to help me make friends.

Danny M. was in the rest of my classes. So I am Dani D. in those classes, too.

I pretended it didn't bother me. I didn't want everyone to think I'm a crybaby. It's the same reason I can't talk about my parents. A couple of the kids were nice to me. Rachel from my Social Studies class let me sit next to her at lunch. But it was not like at home. No one asked about my weekend. No one talked to me about who got voted off on *Dance For It!*

I tried to eat my sandwich. It was hard to swallow.

But then three girls walked in to the cafeteria.

Everyone smiled at them. Or called their names. Or waved at them. Or tried to get them to sit next to them.

It was like they were movie stars.

I kind of saw why these girls were popular. They walked like nothing bothered them. And they looked so happy. The girl in the middle had this huge smile—like today was the best day ever.

"Who are they?" I asked Rachel.

"Oh, that's Hailey," Rachel said. She pointed to the girl in the middle. Hailey is the girl with the big smile. "And that's Tasha. And that's Priya. They are all in drama club. Hailey is super talented. She gets the lead in every school play. And Tasha and Priya are in all the plays, too. Everyone likes them."

And here is where I lied.

"Oh, that's cool," I said. I said it like I didn't care. But I did care. "I used to be in all the plays at my old school, too."

"Really?" another girl at my table asked. "You were in drama club?"

"Oh, yeah," I said.

Here is the truth. I don't even know if my old school *had* a drama club. Maybe it did? I never asked.

"Were you good at it?" the girl asked. "Were you the lead in plays?"

"Oh, yeah," I said. "All the time."

Here is the truth. I've never been in a play before.

But I let them all think it. I let them all think that I used to be a drama club star. That I used to be popular.

"Wow, Dani D," Rachel said. "That's really cool."

I didn't even mind that Rachel called me Dani D. She said it like Dani D. was a cool person.

So the fact that I am not a drama club star now has to be a *total secret*.

Dad always makes plans for his job. He says it's important to know what you are going to do.

So I made a plan for how I would act at school today.

First, I got Mom to let me wear her nice black sweater.

She thought that was funny at first. She laughed and said, "Dani, it won't even fit you!"

It totally *did* fit me. And then Mom got all sad. She started talking about how I was "growing up so fast." She kept hugging me. I was almost late for school.

totally fits!

Moms are weird sometimes.

When I got to school I stood outside the doors for a moment. I tried to picture the way Hailey walked. I tried to see how Tasha smiled. I tried to imagine what it felt like to be them.

It worked.

The bell rang. I walked into class just like Hailey does. Chin up. Head high. I smiled just like Tasha smiles. As big as I could.

And four girls smiled back at me.

I kept smiling all morning. One of the girls walked next to me on the way to science class. I didn't tell her about my parents. I talked about rehearsing with drama club friends at my old school.

"That sounds like so much fun!" the girl said. And then she begged me to be her partner in class.

Even Danny M. didn't make fun of me. He ignored me. But he didn't make fun of me.

Before lunch, I hung out at the bulletin board by the theater. I tried to pretend I belonged there. I kept smiling. I waited.

And then Hailey and Tasha walked up to ME.

"You're Dani D., right?" Hailey asked. Hailey is super pretty. She has long eyelashes and braces with pink rubber bands.

I felt so special. Hailey had heard of *me*. I nodded. "You're Hailey, right?"

Hailey also looked happy that I knew her name. I see why now. Having someone know your name is pretty cool.

"We heard you like theater," Tasha said. Tasha is tall and looks like a ballerina.

"I do!" I said. "I *love* theater. It's so much fun."

By that point, I was starting to even believe myself.

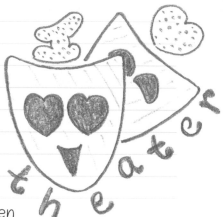

I told Hailey and Tasha about all the plays I was in at my old school. Well, I told them about the plays I was pretending I had been in. They got really excited.

"We're going to be doing a new show here soon," Tasha said. "We need more people. You should try out."

They kept talking to me. They laughed when I made a joke.

They asked me questions.

And then Hailey asked, "Do you want to sit with us at lunch?"

YES!!! Yes, I wanted to sit with them at lunch!

Hailey and Tasha's lunch table was full of kids. And they all wanted to talk to me, too. Hailey is really nice. And Tasha is so much fun. I know they are both going to be my new best friends.

My plan *worked*.

I only thought of Emily Grace and my other friends from home like five times today. I only missed them a little. I didn't even care that I was pretending to be a new me.

I felt happy.

I wasn't worried about Mom and Dad. I wasn't sad. It was actually easy to smile.

It felt true. It felt like maybe I was a new me.

And who knows? Maybe I actually *am* a new me now. Maybe I really am Dani D.—the happy, popular girl. Maybe I'm the girl who has no worries.

Maybe.

Today, I almost felt brave again.

Almost.

It's easier to be brave when you are not alone. It's easier to be brave when you have friends. And I have friends now. Or at least I'm making friends. Hailey and Tasha and Priya and the other girls *aren't* friends yet. I have to remember that. Because I almost messed up.

At lunch Priya complained about her little brother. He is only five. He likes to try on Priya's shoes. That means he usually ruins them.

"My parents are so annoying," Priya said. "They let my brother get away with everything."

Then she asked me if I had a little brother.

I said no.

Then Hailey told a funny story about her older sister.

"Do you have an older sister, Dani D.?" she asked.

I said no.

Then Tasha said her parents were annoying, too. "They never let me do anything. Are your parents annoying, Dani D.?"

"Yeah, totally annoying," I said. That's true. They are VERY annoying. "Especially when they fight—"

I made myself stop talking. It was too late. Everyone at the table was staring at me. Hailey looked confused. Tasha looked worried. Priya looked mad that no one wanted to hear more about her brother.

So I laughed. It was a fake laugh. But it was a laugh. I said, "Especially when they fight over who gets the last piece of cake. Parents are so weird."

Everyone else laughed, too. And Tasha told a funny story about her parents at Thanksgiving. I tried to get it together. I still can't believe I almost gave myself away. I would have lost everything. No one wants to be friends with a sad girl who is worried about her parents. They only want to be friends with funny, popular me.

I hope no one remembers it tomorrow.

What if they do?

I CAN'T mess up again.

Oh! Hailey just texted me! I'm in my room writing this and she texted me!

She wants to know if I can come to a sleepover at her house. This weekend! All the girls from the lunch table are going to be there. I'll get to meet some girls I don't even know yet.

OMG! I can't believe it. *She invited me to a sleepover.*

This is amazing. I just asked Mom, and she says I can go. Well, at first she asked a MILLION questions. She keeps trying to get me to join this craft club at school. And they have a meeting on Friday.

"You loved making crafts with Emily Grace," Mom said. "You should try out craft club. You might make new friends."

I told Mom I WAS making friends.

She sighed. "I meant friends with people you have things in common with. Do you even like acting, Dani?"

I said yes, of course I did. And then I asked if she could let me buy a new pair of pajamas. (My old pajamas are too short. They look like something a little kid would wear.)

And Mom did NOT like that at all. "There's nothing wrong with your old pajamas!" she said. "Why are you trying so hard to impress these new friends? Is that why your hair looks different, too?"

My hair does NOT look different. I just put it back in a high ponytail. Like Hailey does. That's all.

But FINALLY — she said I could go!

This sleepover is going to be perfect. I'm going to make even more friends. All I have to do is keep acting the same way I do at school. I just need to be the new Dani D. I won't mention my family at all. I don't even need to be brave. I only need to be like Tasha and Hailey.

I've totally got this.

how Hailey does it

Friday, November 9

Hailey's sleepover is the best party ever.

Her house is so much fun. Hailey's mom teaches theater at the college. She's really funny—and not in an embarrassing way. Hailey's family is all into theater. Her sister was even in a *commercial.* She got to stand in a pumpkin patch and tell people to come pick pumpkins. Hailey wants to be in movies someday. I think she will be.

I'm writing this in Hailey's bathroom. (Even her bathroom is nice. Grandma's bathroom has wallpaper with kittens on it. Hailey's does not.) I had to take a break from being Dani D. Tasha asked me about my old school, and I forgot to talk about drama club. I almost told her about the crafts Emily Grace and I made.

That would have been a really, really big problem.

So now I am in the bathroom reminding myself—THIS IS A TOTAL SECRET. I can't tell anyone the truth!

Okay, I feel better now.

We've been watching movies. Before that, we danced in Hailey's living room. I love to dance. Hailey put on music, and I just started moving. Tasha thought it was great. She got up and danced with me. And then everyone danced.

I laughed so much my stomach hurts now.

Of course, that might also be because of all the popcorn and candy I ate during the movie.

Hailey wants to play games next. That will probably be Truth or Dare. I will have to pick dare, of course. I can't pick truth! So many bad things could happen.

Oh! Hailey just knocked on the door. I guess I'm taking too long in here.

"Are you coming, Dani D.?" she's asking. "We want to play improv games now."

Improv? That's a funny word. I've never even heard of improv before. I asked Hailey what she meant, and she laughed.

"You know. Theater games," she said. "Didn't you play improv at your old school?"

Uh-oh.

"Oh, yeah, of course we did!" I said. "I thought you meant something else."

I can't see her face. So I don't know if she believes me.

I hope she believes me.

"Hurry up," she said. "This will be so much fun!"

My heart is pounding. I am so nervous. I don't know what improv means. I have never played a theater game before. I have been lying all week. But I don't know how to pretend this. I don't know how to pretend to play a game I've never heard of.

I am going to have to, though. I can't tell Hailey I don't know what improv means. I can't even Google it. My phone is in my bag in the living room. I am just going to have to keep pretending.

It will be okay. I will write it down now so that I will remember.

Don't tell anyone the truth!!

You are a drama star!!

You can do this!

YOU HAVE TO DO THIS!

I have no choice. I have to try. I have to keep pretending.

If I don't, I will lose all my new friends.

Still Friday

It turns out improv is a way of playing pretend.

You would think by now that I would be good at playing pretend.

But I am not good at improv. I am not good at acting. I am not good at drama club games.

I am a fake.

I ruined everything.

I am back in the bathroom now. I'm waiting for Mom to come pick me up. I told Hailey's mom I wanted to go home. She said that was okay.

It doesn't feel okay. It feels like everything is ending.

At first, the games were fun. Everyone was just laughing and being silly.

We started with a "warm-up." We had to repeat sentences that are hard to say over and over. These are called "tongue twisters." The other girls noticed that I didn't know any tongue twisters.

I said that's because my old drama club said *different* tongue twisters.

Hailey got excited. "Oh! I love learning new tongue twisters. You have to teach us!"

I said that I forgot them all.

Then we had to pick a card out of a hat. I was so confused. I was going to copy Tasha and see what she did. But then Hailey said I was the "guest" and could go first.

I pulled my card out. All it said was "zookeeper" and "park bench."

I stared at the card for a long time. Everyone was staring at me. I had no idea what to do.

Finally I asked, "Is this a new game of Go Fish or something?"

Hailey laughed. But then she saw that I wasn't joking. She said I was supposed to pretend to be what was written on the card. Then the others were supposed to guess what the card said.

I tried pretending to be a zookeeper. No one guessed what I was.

Then we played *more* games where we had to pretend. The games were funny when other kids did them. Tasha made everyone laugh so hard. And Priya is really clever.

But every time it was my turn they had to explain the games to me again. Or I didn't do something right. Or I just looked stupid instead of funny.

The other girls looked really confused.

"Wow, Dani D.," Tasha said. "Your old drama club didn't play *any* games?"

And then I did the worst thing I could do.

I told the truth.

"I've never been in drama club before," I said. "Never."

I don't know why I said it. I didn't mean to. I didn't want to. It felt like all my lies were bubbling up inside of me. Like they were coming out whether I wanted them to or not.

"I wasn't a drama club star in my old school," I said. "I wasn't popular. I wasn't the lead in all the plays. I've never even been in a play before. I made it all up."

"I don't get it," Hailey said. "You were lying to us? The whole time?"

"Why?" Tasha asked.

Everyone in the room was staring at me. Everyone was waiting for me to say something.

So I told another secret.

"Because my parents might get a divorce," I said.

I've never actually said that word out loud before. I don't want them to get a divorce. I want my parents to get back together. I want to think they are only just "taking a break."

"They fight all the time," I said. It was like my mouth wouldn't stop talking. "My dad is far away. And I miss my dad. I miss all my friends."

No one moved. They all kept staring at me. None of them understood. None of their parents were "taking a break." None of them moved.

So I did something even worse.

I started crying.

I cried big, fat, blubbery tears. Crybaby tears. Hailey's eyes widened. Tasha took a step back. Priya's mouth fell open.

And I ran out of the room.

I ran to the bathroom. I locked the bathroom door. And I cried some more.

Hailey's mom came and checked on me after a little while. Not Hailey. She asked if I was okay. That's when I told her I wanted to go home.

I'm not okay. I'm a liar and a fake and scared of everything.

And now everybody knows it.

Later Friday

I am in Mom's car now. We are driving back to my grandparents' house.

No one at the party even said goodbye to me.

Everyone there will tell everyone else at school. No one is ever going to be my friend now.

Mom keeps asking me what's wrong.

"You'll feel better if you talk about it, Dani," she's saying. "Believe me."

I don't believe her. I don't think there's any way I'm going to feel better.

"Can you at least stop writing in that diary so we can talk?" she asks.

I don't want to talk. I want to keep writing down what she says in my diary. So that's what I do.

Mom keeps sighing. A LOT. She's driving now.
But she keeps looking at me like she wants me
to talk.

I keep writing.

Then Mom says, "Your dad called me earlier."

This almost makes me talk. My parents
haven't spoken to each other on the phone since
Mom and I left. This is all part of their "break."

"He is worried about you," Mom says. "I told
him I was worried about you, too."

WHY WOULD SHE DO THAT!?

I ask Mom that.

Her answer is stupid.

"Because I *am* worried about you, Dani,"
she says.

I ask her why she's worried. Her reason is
even MORE stupid.

"You've been trying really, really hard to make new friends," she says. "Maybe a little too hard."

"Why don't you want me to make friends?" I ask. My mom doesn't get ANYTHING. "Friends are really important!"

"I know friends are important," Mom says. "I want you to have friends."

She has a funny way of showing that.

"Dani, I do," she's saying. "But I'm worried about how you are going about making friends. I worry you are losing yourself."

Uh-oh. I didn't tell Mom I was pretending to be a drama club star. Just that I was trying it out. Does Mom know I've been lying?

"What do you mean?" I ask. "How am I losing myself?"

"You wear different clothes now. You talk differently. You have new hobbies. Sometimes it's like you are becoming a new person. I miss the old Dani."

I sink lower into my seat. "What's wrong with changing? Don't people change?"

That's what Mom had said when she and Dad decided on their "break." She said that they had "changed." If they changed, why can't I?

"Of course people change!" Mom says. "People change all the time. And you are growing up. Change is natural. Change is important. But I worry that you are forcing yourself to change."

HELLO, I'M
Changing

Mom pulls the car into the driveway. But we don't get out yet. She looks at me instead.

"I don't want you to think you need to change for people to like you," she says.

Whatever. Mom obviously doesn't remember what it's like to be in middle school

"I think you are afraid to be yourself," Mom says. "That's what I told your dad, anyway."

WHAT??? SHE TOLD DAD WHAT???

Super Late Friday

It's true. Mom TOLD Dad I was afraid!!!

I don't know how she could do this. I don't know how she could TELL DAD I WAS AFRAID.

My parents can't even talk about who is supposed to buy milk from the store. They get in fights. But NOW Mom talks to Dad? NOW she tells him things? And she tells him I'M AFRAID?!?!?

This is the worst thing that could happen. This is almost worse than what happened at Hailey's party. I did NOT want Dad to find out I wasn't brave. The whole point of this was to find friends so I wouldn't be scared. So I could be brave again, and Dad could still be proud of me. So he could still be proud of me even though he's far away.

And now everything is RUINED!

Saturday, November 10

All my total secrets are not secrets anymore.

None of them. My diary was supposed to keep everyone from knowing. But it didn't. Everyone found out I'm not a drama club star. My dad found out I'm not brave.

I made everything worse.

I messed up big time.

I've been in my room all day. Mom keeps trying to get me to talk. She tells me my dad is on the phone. He wants to talk to me. But I tell her I just want to be alone.

Because I do. I want to be alone. I don't want to see how disappointed Dad is. I don't want to tell Mom I lied. I don't want to think about how I won't have any friends Monday in school. I want to pretend that Friday night didn't happen.

"never, ever, ever leaving my room" slippers

I try pretending that. But then I remember—I actually stink at pretending. That's what got me in trouble in the first place. So I'm just going to stay here. Alone.

Sunday, November 11

Being alone stinks.

Mom made me come out of my room for dinner last night. And for breakfast and lunch today. And she made me do my homework. But other than that I have been in my room Alone.

I hate it.

It turns out I don't actually want to be alone anymore. I've felt alone for a long, long time. Even before all this happened. I have felt alone ever since we got here. Ever since we left home. Ever since Mom and Dad took a break.

I haven't talked to anyone about my feelings. I didn't tell Emily Grace I was sad. I didn't tell Mom I was lonely. I didn't tell Dad I was scared. I didn't want any of them to know those things. I only wrote my feelings down in my diary.

But Dad knows the truth now. He knows I'm scared. So I might as well tell him all the rest. He is already disappointed that I'm not brave— he might as well also know that I'm a liar. And a fake. It can't really make it that much worse. And then I could talk to him.

I'm going to call Dad.

Sunday night

I forgot my dad wears glasses at night.

I don't know how I forgot that. I guess I always picture him in his uniform. In my head, he's always the way he looks when he gets home from work. But at night my dad wears glasses to read.

It's a really strange thing to forget.

He was wearing his glasses when he answered my video chat. He had on my favorite green hoodie. He was drinking out of his favorite mug. And he smiled when he saw me. Like I was the best thing he'd seen all day.

"Dani! I've been trying to call you all week. Didn't you get my messages?"

He looked sad. He looked lonely. I didn't mean to make my dad sad or lonely. I only wanted to wait to talk to him when I had friends again. I wanted to feel happy so I could act brave. So I could be the Dani my dad needs me to be.

45

But I'm not. And pretending to be a new me has only made everything worse.

"Dad," I said. "I have something to tell you."

I told him everything. All about pretending at school. About having to share a name with Danny M. I told him I'm NOT brave. At all. I told him I'm so afraid. I'm afraid to be myself. I'm afraid no one will like me. I'm afraid the only friends I will ever make are far, far away. I'm afraid of all the fears I have.

And then I waited for him to look worse than sad. I waited for him to look disappointed in me.

But he didn't look disappointed. At all.

Instead he said something that completely surprised me.

"You are still the bravest girl I know, Dani," he said. "Hands down. Look at what you are doing — starting a new school, making new friends, moving, living with your grandparents. All of that takes guts. Being brave doesn't mean you won't ever be afraid. It means doing things when you *are* afraid."

I got tears in my eyes. I had to blink hard. He waited until I calmed down.

"I'm so proud of you," he said. "So, so proud. Making new friends is going to take time."

"It's just so hard," I told him.

"Most things in life worth having are hard," Dad said. "You just have to keep trying."

I thought about what Dad said for a long, long time after he hung up.

I decided Dad is right. I'm going to keep trying to make friends. But this time I'm going to be honest about what I like. I might even still try drama—parts of it were kind of fun. But I won't say I'm a star. It doesn't even matter if I share a name with Danny M. Dani D. is a completely different person than Danny M.

I'm not going to be a new person. I'm just going to be me.

Dad was right. I had to be brave to go to school today. Being yourself in middle school is HARD.

I still did it anyway!!!!!!!!

I even wore my old clothes. Mom was happy about that. She didn't like that I kept borrowing her stuff. It felt so nice to wear my favorite skirt again. And my bright blue shirt just made me happy.

The hardest part was walking into school. It felt like the first day all over again. I was so afraid everyone would know about what happened at Hailey's party. I was afraid they would all be laughing at me. Or that they would think I was stupid AND a fake.

But then I remembered how Dad said being brave is doing things when you are afraid. So I walked in.

No one laughed
at me. The drama club
girls weren't even in the
hallway. That part was a little
sad They normally waited for me.
We walked to first period together.

Today I had to walk by myself.

I did it, though. I walked by myself. I didn't
tell any more lies about drama club. I didn't
pretend to be someone else.

But I DID still smile at people. And kids
still smiled back at me. Even without me talking
about drama club!

It made me think I had been wrong this whole time. Maybe I never needed to pretend to be a drama club star. Maybe some kids never cared about that. Maybe I only needed to smile and be friendly. Maybe other kids are scared, too. Maybe I could've been myself the whole time.

Maybe.

I saw Hailey, Tasha, and Priya at lunch. I thought they would all be mad at me. Or that they would have told all the other kids I was a fake. Instead they just looked sad. They looked like I had hurt their feelings.

I probably did. No one likes being lied to.

I had to REALLY be brave then. This was harder than walking into school. This was even harder than saying goodbye to Emily Grace. I wanted to pretend again. I wanted to just go sit somewhere else. I wanted to ignore them.

But instead I walked up to them. "Hi, guys," I said. Hailey, Tasha, and Priya all looked at each other. Then they looked back at me. I wished I were anywhere else.

"I'm really sorry I lied," I said. "I know it was wrong. I really wanted to make friends. I thought you all would like me if you thought I was good at drama. I know it doesn't make sense. I just wanted you to know I'm sorry."

It was the scariest thing I've ever done. But I did it anyway. So maybe Dad is right. Maybe I am brave.

I don't think any of the girls really get why I lied. But they were mostly nice about it. Hailey shrugged and said, "I guess it's okay. I mean, I get that you didn't mean to hurt our feelings. Just don't lie again, okay?"

I promised I wouldn't lie again. And she smiled a little. But then she started talking to Tasha and Priya.

I don't know that any of them are ever going to be my new best friend. But that's okay.

Best friends take time.

After lunch Danny M. followed me back to class. He kept yelling "Dani DDDDDDDDDDDDDDDD." Like there were a million Ds in my name. He thought it was so funny. He kept laughing.

Finally I said, "Whatever, Danny M. We have the same nickname. GET OVER IT."

He turned bright red. And then he left me alone for the rest of the day. It was amazing.

But my name IS Dani D. And sometimes I mess up. And sometimes I do things even though I'm afraid. And all of that is okay.

I'm not a new me. I'm just me.

And this time, that's NOT a total secret.

Want to Keep Reading?

Turn the page for a sneak peek
at the next book in the series.

9781538381977

Tuesday, January 8

Grandma keeps telling me to be quiet.

"Dani," she called up the stairs just now. "Can you please turn your music down? Your grandpa is watching his show."

She *always* thinks I'm too loud. But I'm NOT. Not *really*. I just like to dance in my room. That was no problem in my old room in my old house. But now that Mom and I live with Grandma and Grandpa, it is a PROBLEM.

So I put on my new headphones. Mom just bought them for me. She thought that would solve the noise problem. I danced wearing my headphones instead of playing music out loud. But Grandma STILL knocked on my bedroom door.

"You're making the ceiling shake, Dani," she said. "Can you please stop dancing? Don't you have homework?"

I finished my homework already. That's why I was dancing.

Grandma didn't care. She wanted to make dinner without the ceiling shaking. I asked if I could dance after dinner. But she said that's when Grandpa likes to read.

I can't win.

Now I'm writing in my diary instead of dancing. I like to write in my diary. That part is okay. But I also like to dance. I don't like to sit still all day long. I have to sit still in school. I have to sit still to do homework.

Sometimes, I just want to move around.

Mom says it's just for a little bit. I have to be "flexible." That really means she wants me to just do whatever Grandma wants without complaining.

But it's not fair. My mom and dad are "taking a break." Mom and I have lived with Grandma and Grandpa for two whole months. We moved away from my old town. I go to a new school now. In school, I have to share my name with Danny M. I go by "Dani D." now. Danny M. is the most annoying boy EVER. My old friends are far away. My dad is far away.

And now Grandma wants me to be quiet.

I think Grandma and I need to take a "break."

Here is everything I can't do at Grandma's house:

- Make extra chocolaty brownies in the kitchen. Dad and I used to make extra-chocolaty brownies all the time. But Grandma always says "no" when I ask to make them here. Mom can't cook here, either. Mom likes to cook. But Grandma doesn't like it when anyone else uses her stove. This makes Mom sad.

- Watch *Dance For It!*. Grandma says I can't watch TV at night. The only TV is in the living room. That's where Grandpa likes to read. Now I don't know who gets voted off until WAY after everyone else! I watch clips on my phone. But that is NOT THE SAME. I already know who is going home!

- Hang out with other kids. I can't have anyone from school over. And there are no kids in Grandma's neighborhood. Only old people live here.

ABOUT THE AUTHOR

J.M. Klein is a former journalist who has lived all around the country and moved half a dozen times. Like Dani, she learned how to make new friends and tried out for the school play. She didn't make that play, but she did develop a lifelong love of theater and now has good friends in many states. She's always written in diaries and journals, the contents of which are still totally secret.

Check out more books at:

www.west44books.com

An imprint of Enslow Publishing

WEST **44** BOOKS™